House by the river

*Special thanks to Monika Keano for taking
this journey with me.
Without her vision this book would not have
come to life in its present form.*

Copyright © 2000 by Tomek Bogacki
All rights reserved
Distributed in Canada by Douglas & McIntyre Ltd.
Color separations by Hong Kong Scanner Arts
Printed and bound in the United States of America by Berryville Graphics
Art direction and design by Monika Keano
First edition, 2000

Library of Congress Cataloging-in-Publication Data
Bogacki, Tomasz.
    My first garden / Tomek Bogacki. — 1st ed.
      p.
    "Frances Foster books."
    Summary: Inspired by hearing that a garden used to grow in the
yard in front of his house, a boy recreates it with loving care.
    ISBN 0-374-32518-9
    [1. Gardens—Fiction.]   I. Title.
PZ7.B6357825Mt 2000
[E]—dc21   99-24503

My First
GARDEN

Tomek Bogacki

Frances Foster Books

Farrar Straus Giroux

New York

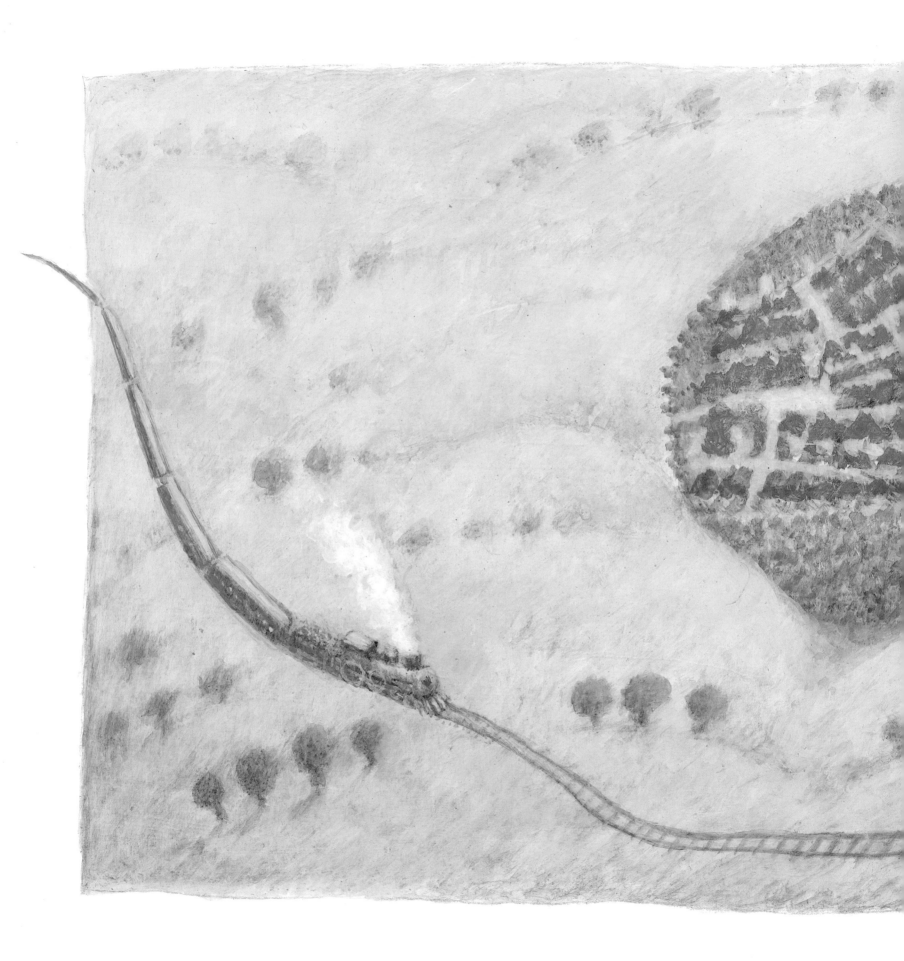

The train was moving slowly through the green countryside. A town in the distance made me think of the town where I was born. It lay in a wide river valley surrounded by rolling hills. With its red-roofed houses it always reminded me of a big bed of flowers.

I remembered when I was a boy waiting at the train station for my father.

The house I lived in was at the edge of town, on the bank of the river. From the window of my room I could see the entire town with its maze of narrow streets and rows of houses.

The house was big, and the town was small. That's what everyone said. To me it seemed the other way around.

My mother always put fresh flowers in the dining room.

The attic was my favorite place. I spent hours there reading, drawing, daydreaming.

The kitchen was often filled with the smell of freshly baked apple pie.

My brother played the piano every afternoon. He was practicing for his first concert.

My sister liked to listen to him play.

I liked to visit my grandfather in his study.

I kept some of my toys in the attic.

The pantry was our best hiding place.

The cellar was the place we didn't like to go to alone.

We lived on the top floor of the house. I knew every corner in it, its stairways, rooms, alcoves, and hallways . . . all its secret hideouts from the cellar to the attic. But I knew only a few of the streets in my town.

The school was just around the corner from my house.

I could buy ice cream or pastries in the small bakery on my way home from school . . .

. . . and I liked to stop and look at the colorful book covers in the window of the bookstore.

"Stop that noise!"

called Mrs. Nowakoska.

"Take your game somewhere else!" Mrs. Lewandoska screamed at us.

After school, I spent most of the time with the other children who lived in our house. We liked to play in the cobblestone courtyard behind the house, but we always made too much noise, or messed up the laundry drying on the clothesline, or somehow threw a ball right into someone's window.

We often wished the cobblestone yard was just for us.

Sometimes we grew tired of all the games we knew. We'd play them over and over, and we didn't know what else to do.

Then one day I got a bike. It had belonged to my older brother, but now it was mine.

Church Street was uphill.

Water Street led to the river.

Narrow Street was downhill.

I went around the City Hall on my way to the park.

The park was one of my favorite places.

Long Street was the longest street in town.

I discovered new streets every day.

I rode my new-old bike everywhere. The town seemed to get smaller and smaller the farther I went.

Every Friday I would ride to the train station to meet my father coming back from the big city, where he worked.

Green Street led out of town.

The house at the end of town

Sliding down the banister was almost always fun . . .

I rode my bike to school even though
it was just around the corner.

In biology class we watched as tiny green plants grew from bean seeds.

"Can we fall off the earth?" we wondered in geography class when the teacher explained how gravity works.

In school I liked biology, geography, and, perhaps best of all, my drawing class, but I couldn't wait to get back on my bike . . .

We learned all about perspective in our drawing class.

One day after school I rode my bike out of town. The road stretched before me looking exactly like the perspective we'd learned in our drawing class. I came to a grassy meadow filled with wildflowers. I liked them so much better than the cobblestones of our courtyard.

I brought a big bouquet of wildflowers home. My grandfather helped me put them in a vase in our dining room.

"Do you think we could have flowers in our yard?" I asked.

"Oh, yes," he said. "There was a beautiful garden here once, around the well. A long time ago, when I was a boy like you."

My grandparents going for their afternoon walk

I wondered if there were any seeds left from my grandfather's garden. I watered the stones, hoping that something would grow there again.

I took my bike and went for a ride, as I did every day. As I rode my bike I thought about the garden that had once grown in our yard, and I imagined the courtyard filled with flowers again.

Suddenly
I realized that
I was on a road
I'd never been on
before. I passed many
fences and gates. The
houses were fewer and
fewer. I wasn't sure where
I was. I stopped in front
of an open gate. I got
off my bike and
went in,
and I found
myself inside a
beautiful garden.

"Do you like flowers?"
I heard a voice behind me.
I turned and I saw a lady
in a big straw hat holding
a watering can.

"Every flower in my garden has its own story," she said. "And, you know, a long time ago there were just cobblestones here," she added with a smile.

The afternoon went by quickly as we walked around this magical place.

When I got home, it was almost dark. There was no one in the yard. I opened the toolshed. Everything I needed was there. So I began to work.

What is he doing?

I brought sticks to build a fence.

I removed stone after stone from around the well.

What is he doing?

I got flower seedlings at the market.

I dug and raked, raked and dug, to make circle patches.

I planted the seedlings in the soil.

I watered them every day.

What is he doing?

As the days passed by, I watched for any weeds growing.

One day I saw the first tiny flowers.

At last the garden was in full bloom.

Everyone liked the garden
and wanted to help.

Now we could play in our courtyard as much as we wanted.
No one seemed to mind anymore.

Even Mrs. Lewandoska and Mrs. Nowakoska sat for hours on a little bench in front of the garden, talking.

The train stopped at a very small station at the edge of the forest. Through the window I could see my son waiting for me beside the train tracks as I used to wait for my father.

On our way home, we talked about
my son's first garden—the one he
was making himself.

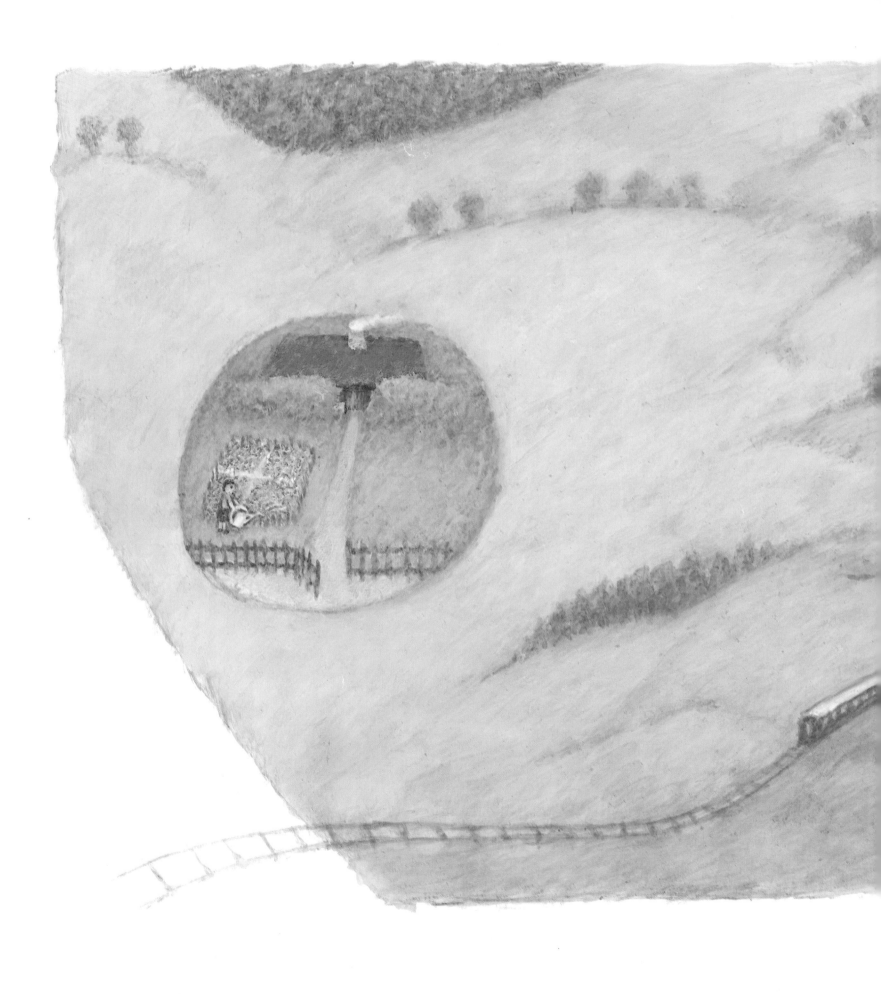

The train moved slowly through
the green countryside . . .